Your Shame
My Shame

Jacqueline McClenaghan

Copyright

First published in 2019

All rights reserved

@Jacqueline McClenaghan, 2019

The right of Jacqueline McClenaghan to be identified as author of this work has been asserted in accordance with Section 77 of the Copyright, Designs and Patents Act 1988

This book is copyright material and must not be copied, reproduced, transferred, distributed, leased, licensed or publicly performed or used in any way except as specifically permitted in writing by the publisher, as allowed under the terms and conditions under which it was purchased or as strictly permitted by applicable copyright law. Any unauthorised distribution or use of this text may be a direct infringement of the author's and publisher's rights, and those responsible may be liable in law accordingly

This book is with thanks to

My animacara, Mary.

My beloved Father and Son.

My family and my 'truly' friends – they know who they are.

Your Shame My Shame

CONTENTS

Dancing from Despair	7/8
The Pyjamas	9 – 11
The Black Trench Coat	12 – 16
The Swanky Coat	17 – 20
The Dexter	21 – 23
The Swing Coat	24 – 26
The Blazer	27 – 32
Without a Coat	33 – 37
Bill's Story	38 – 52
Janine's Story	53 – 68
Wits' End	69/70
The Widower	71 – 75
Her Story	76 – 105
Peter	106 – 119
His Story	120 – 128

Jacqueline McClenaghan

Your Shame My Shame

Dancing from Despair

Jacqueline McClenaghan

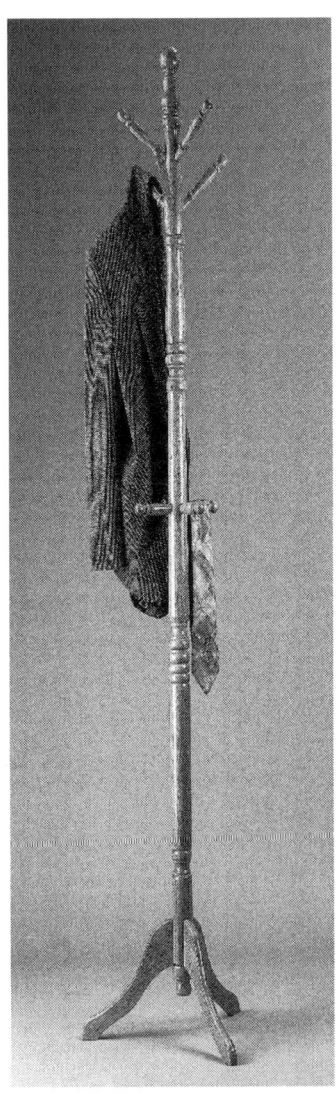

THE PYJAMAS

Mother and daughter are both in their pyjamas. The little girl looks down at hers and looks away, she knows that if she starts to count the rabbits her eyes will close. She examines her Mother's instead. Yellow with dots, washed out, faded with a few burn holes.

It was called 'moquette' this nobbly stuff, which prickled her legs, as she perched on the arm of her Mother's chair. It was foggy and beginning to get dark outside. The street lamps were lit. They sat looking out of the window for a very long time. No words were spoken, and the atmosphere was like a big stretched elastic band about to snap.

Mother took another cigarette from her silver packet, she lit it with a match, she seemed to be chewing on the cigarette and blowing smoke at the same time. The little girl watched all this from the corner of her eye, so as not to draw attention to herself. Mother began to swing her crossed leg backward and forward, backward and forward; it seemed to mesmerise the child. She drew her eyes away, it was putting her to sleep. Mother would be so very angry if she fell asleep.

She longed for her bed, which dipped in the middle and the soft groove of her pillow. When Daddy was home early he filled her a hot water bottle, only he called it 'the jar.' There would be no jar tonight. They continued to look down the street, no, Mother called it 'the drive'. Still there was no one to be seen.

She didn't know what to say to her Mother, afraid of any angry response, she searched frantically for some words, and when none would come, she continued to sit mute, rigid and cold on the arm of the chair. It was dark now, lights were on in other houses. Mr Thompson was taking his dog for a walk. It was a lovely wee dog, she wished it was time for school so that she could pet the wee dog, and it would lick her hand. She wished she had a wee dog. The tears were coming now almost choking with anxiety, she had to think of something quickly, so that they wouldn't spill over. Turning her head slightly to the left she focused with all her might on the piano. It was ugly. She could see no point in cleaning the keys with PLJ. It wouldn't make it pretty. There, the tears had been swallowed, and Mother hadn't noticed.

"There he is" the words made her jump, they seemed strange in this room which had been silent for so long. Peering anxiously out of the window, and although it was dark, she could see clearly that there was no indicator popping out of the side of the car. It wove its way unsteadily towards the house. She felt sick, her stomach churned and gurgled, as she stood beside her Mother watching the big black car being reversed into the driveway. Forward again, and back, and almost hitting the pillar. Revving the engine, forward and back, bit by bit it was slowly going in. Now it was time, "Come on, Margaret," her Mother spoke again. She followed her Mother out of the sitting room, into the hall and towards the kitchen. Out of the door and into the cold dark night air. To 'help' her Father out of the car.

THE BLACK TRENCH COAT

Margaret made her way into the store with her pay packet inside a purse which was in a zipped compartment in her shoulder bag. Couldn't be too careful, thieving gits had stolen her purse last month. That wasn't going to happen again.

She was oblivious of the admiring looks she attracted. Slim, strident, and with long straight hair, (the girls in work called it 'strawberry blonde'). How could she know what a lovely girl she was? Her mother had never told her. Trying on the black belted coat she turned this way and that, imagining the different ways it could be worn. Jeans and polo neck, or dressed up a bit for work. She had to have it, never mind saving for the wedding. Making her way to the till, the sales assistant said, "We were watching you trying on the coat, we agreed that it was made for you. It looks great with your lovely hair."

"Thank you, you're very kind," said Margaret blushing to the roots of her 'lovely hair'.

Making for the exit with her coat, she ran to catch the bus to her parents house.

With a feeling of dread she got off at the bus stop. No matter what she did or how hard she tried, it was never good enough. Her Mother twisted her words and deeds or sneered at her. Margaret could not understand, how could she rub along with Margaret's sister and brother, but not with her?

A determination set in, the woman was to be pitied. Margaret was not going to allow the pleasure of the new coat and her wedding plans to be ruined. She couldn't wait to be married and away from her Mother, she shuddered as she went through the back door.

An hour later she was sitting at the table with her parents.

"Where's the other two?" asked her Daddy.

"Young Bill is at David's house for tea and Janine is staying over at Elaine's house. They can go to school together tomorrow."

Daddy raised his eyebrows, he was of the old school

and didn't understand these sleep-overs and eating with strangers. Fields and bicycles in his day. Margaret knew they were escaping the atmosphere in the house and found it easier to be in other people's houses.

The situation had become too big, no one spoke of it, therefore, it didn't exist. There remained a thin veneer of what made a happy family. Meal times, Daddy in the garden, the other two bickering over who would go to the shop. Underneath there simmered a sense of despair and doom.

Ah well, time to do the dishes and make the tea.

"Do you want tea in the living room?"

"That's grand and I can watch the news."

"I'll have mine in there too," said her Mother, shuffling in those gruesome slippers, toward the living room.

Margaret, waiting for the kettle to boil, could hear her Mother pleading:

"Sure go up 'the hill' and bring the shopping trolley."

"No, I haven't the money and I've work in the morning."

"You could ask Margaret, she always has a few pounds tucked away. She won't mind if you ask her."

Well, yes she would fumed Margaret, there would be no hand-outs to knock them senseless on booze.

Bringing the tea in she said "It's only a cup of tea; I've no money for biscuits. I'm going on now, out to meet Ben."

"Ah, the groom to be, discussing the plans?" asked her Dad.

"Yes, we've paid a deposit for the reception, and the flowers are paid for. You've to try on your top hat and tails next week."

"Sure I'll look a right berk, still, if that's what you two have set your mind to."

Mother, shaking her foot backward and forward could hardly keep a lid on her mounting temper.

"That's ages away. It's tonight I'm thinking of. Those tablets have me parched, what do you say, Bill?"

"No, I'll walk you to the bus stop, Margaret,"

"Ah, for God's sake, she's not a child. You can get on a bus yourself, can't you?" her Mother asked glaring at her.

"Well, yes, of course I can, but it would be nice to have company," smiled Margaret.

Her Daddy went to get his coat and cap from the coat stand.

Her Mother whispered, so that he wouldn't hear her, "You're a horrible wee bitch, getting him to go out in the cold after a hard day at work. I'm telling you now, I'll make sure you don't have a fancy fairy tale wedding." Margaret could feel spittle on her face, she looked at her in astonishment. Of course if it had been going to get drink, the cold and a hard day at work wouldn't have been thought of. Margaret was tired of trying to make her Mother see sense. She turned on her heel and waited in the hall. Deep breathing, deep breathing; now, do not let her get to you.

"I'm away to the bus with Margaret, won't be long."

No reply.

Margaret linked her Daddy's arm and walked companionably towards the bus stop, watched from behind the curtains by her Mother.

THE SWANKY COAT

Remembering the day he brought it home for her, a green three quarter length coat, and as he called it a "robin hood hat," to match. It was very precious and more so because of the surprise.

Surprise, that he would actually go through the door of a ladies shop. Surprise, that it was exactly right for her. It had once been lovely, like herself she supposed. Photographs of her younger self showed this to be true. Not any more. Drink and pills had ravaged her face and figure. Her lovely shiny hair was like straw. Everything was too much effort, foggy, she could hardly reach her thoughts. The soft thick material had worn thin, the lustre of it long gone and it was shabby. She sat on the bed stroking it, away somewhere else.

"Hello, hello, anybody in?" It was the voice of her eldest

Daughter, Margaret bouncing into the bedroom, "What are you doing with that coat?" "Just remembering the time when your Daddy bought it for me." "Oh, well, it's quite old now, isn't it?"

She wanted to smack her, who was this wee madam? With her 'quite,' and her long beautiful hair.

Looking at her with pity, no it wasn't that; it was contempt, yes, that's what it was. A type of arrogance and defiance.

Billy, her husband, had said that she was totally unreasonable where Margaret was concerned. Worse than that, he'd told her, "If you ever beat that child again, there'll be consequences'. Well, she didn't like the sound of that. It sounded threatening. Billy didn't do threats, so she knew it was serious.

And yet, and yet, yes there it was creeping through her. The raw dislike she often had for this girl. God help her, for she couldn't help herself.

"You mean old like me?" she demanded.

Margaret backed away, fear on her face, but, no she couldn't leave it.

"No, I never said that, and anyway why are you still

wearing that dressing gown?"

"Oh, just get out of my sight," she screeched, so hard that she could feel spittle on her lips.

"Pleasure," the wee bitch retorted, going quickly and quietly downstairs.

She had stopped calling her "Mummy" a long time ago, couldn't remember when that had happened, she just noticed it one day. It was never mentioned, like so many other things.

She just wanted to take another pill and crawl back into bed. When did she get out of it?

Couldn't remember that either.

She got off the bed, and struggled to find her clothes. There they were, hanging off the chair.

She lifted the trousers, smelt them and wrinkled her nose, before stepping into them. Next, her jumper, merino wool did bobble she noticed before she pulled it over her head. She slipped her feet into her comfortable worn slippers. She padded to the bathroom, cleaned her teeth and splashed cold water over her face. Glancing in the mirror, she made do with patting her wispy hair. She didn't linger.

Slowly and with the gait of a woman twice her age, she made her way downstairs.

The task of making the dinner was monumental. Where was the woman who threw together tasty dinners and apple tarts? Where? indeed.

Margaret was chopping the vegetables, the potatoes resting in a pot of water, the chicken was coated in flour. She felt a surge of gratitude towards the girl. Something in her twisted, a ferocious spite and she thought that this was just another way to show her up. She looked around for the pan, how could she forget where she kept the pan? Oh who cared! Let Miss Goody two shoes deal with it.

She shuffled out of the kitchen and into the living room. She fell into the sofa, the springs no longer holding it together. She used to polish the suite with leather spray, the carpet was now shabby and worn and the silver velvet curtains were bunched together so that the faded bits didn't show so much. It was like a seedy old film set.

No pride, that's what these pills had taken from her, and hope. She had no pride and no hope left in her house, herself, or her life.

THE DEXTER

I'm heading home now, tying the belt of the Dexter tight round my middle and turning the collar up.

The coat belonged to my Da, quality.

"Yes, in its day," I can almost hear Margaret saying.

I don't care, it's warm and waterproof. I need to stop at the off licence at the top of the hill, or it'll be hell to pay. The truth is, I don't want to sit in the front room, playing old records and listening to the wife drone on and on. Oblivion can't come quick enough. It's only five weeks 'till the wedding. I've given my mate Jack five hundred pounds to keep for me. A bit of overtime, and, a few sneaky homers. I don't let on, or there wouldn't be a penny to give to the young couple. I dread Margaret leaving the house, oh I know she makes dinners and keeps an eye on the other two. I never forget the morning she came into the kitchen dressed in her uniform. Using her hair to try and hide her battered face.

I looked at the wife, "She refused to eat the good dinner I made."

"Stay off school today pet," I said to her.

Quietly she left the kitchen and headed back upstairs.

"Will I bring Margaret some coffee and toast, dad?" asked wee Janine.

"Yes, ducks, you do that."

Young Bill was oblivious, dipping his 'soldiers' into his boiled egg.

I knew it would probably be better to leave it until I got home that night.

I couldn't.

"A word in the parlour," for once she didn't correct me, just followed meekly.

I closed the door and then I put my hands round her neck. I don't remember all I said, but I do recall how she hissed into my face, "More ways than one to skin a cat, and no matter, the cat doesn't like it, Bill". I recoiled from her and went to work.

After that day I suspect she just got cuter in her torturous ways. Margaret never said a word, but sometimes I would find her gazing into the distance, or considering her Mother as though she were an alien.

Never mind that 'you make your bed and you lie in it,' I won't be lying in that bed much longer.

I'm nearly at the off sales now. I'll keep this up until Margaret has her big day. I hate that house, I don't hate my wife, but she's not the woman I married. I don't understand the spite, the tablets, and the slovenly ways of her.

I feel in my Dexter pocket for a cigarette and sit on the wall outside the off sales to smoke it.

I can smell fish and chips from across the road. I'll get a parcel to bring home when I've bought the drink.

I'll put them in the pocket of my Dexter to keep them warm.

THE SWING COAT

Sometimes my sister and I really do not like each other and sometimes we are really close. Maybe all sisters are like that? I don't know.

She sent me a coat from London. I love to say "My sister sent me this from London". She thinks this is hilarious.

I am close to Mum, but, her and our Margaret can't stand each other. I don't know why, but Mum is vicious to her and Margaret looks at her with real contempt. Our Bill is Mum's wee pet, he gets away with murder.

Da is a bit strict sometimes, doesn't hit us but cuts the tripe out of you.

I'm putting off telling you what happened. Stay with me, let me ramble on a bit.

I have mates who live 'over the bridge'. Margaret says

"they're common as muck". Nothing to do with her, she has a few airs and graces. Told me that she was going to live in a mansion and I could be her cleaning lady. Can't wait for that to happen,

Any excuse and I'm out of the house. I hate it, no, I hate what happens in it. Starting with Mum 'phoning me to school to ask that I come home because she's sick. Sure when is she well? The sitting room – well, welcome to the mad house. Drink, drink and more drink, noise, noise and more noise. Silence, pissed and passed out.

Ok, now you get the picture.

I had escaped, I thought for the day 'over the bridge' to my mates house. I had hardly taken my coat off when my Brother was at the door. He says, "You have to come quick. Mum has taken tablets."

I says, "She's always taking bloody tablets."

I knew I had to go. Running alongside him so puffed I could hardly speak.

In the front door I went, fuming and started to tidy the mess in the sitting room. Cans, brandy bottles, ashes, the usual afternoon refreshment.

I went upstairs and Mum was coming out of the

bathroom. "What have you taken?" I asked her.

"Nothing that will do me any harm" she slurred and staggered into the bedroom.

I went back downstairs and continued to bring the empties into the kitchen. I saw empty tablet bottles and a note beside it.

Margaret and her boyfriend arrived. The boyfriend raced up the stairs and started to give her mouth to mouth. Margaret 'phoned for an ambulance.

I went with her in the ambulance, her lips were purply blue. I felt sick. Was she dead, no no she couldn't be. I thought that maybe I was wrong.

They whisked her away and a nurse brought me to a family room. I sat there alone. A doctor came out, "Your Mother is dead."

I sat there numb. I 'phoned the house and Margaret's boyfriend said that I was to get a taxi and he'd pay for it when I got home.

Oh Jesus, what the hell will happen now?

THE BLAZER

People think children don't understand things, but they understand lots of things.

Sometimes it's just a feeling and sometimes they listen at doors. Well, I do and my mate David does too.

Mum loves me to bits, she calls me 'her wee man,' she loves Janine and hates Margaret.

Da can be strict but fair, he doesn't hit us, he just looks angry or disappointed. I play up a bit to Mum and she'll take my part, so I don't ever really get punished at all.

My mate David and I have loads of fun together, always out and about. Racing our bikes, ringing doorbells and running away, oh, and firing pellets. I have a catapult, I keep it in the inside pocket of my blazer. David's getting one with his pocket money on Friday. We play hide and seek, but one day David hid on the roof of our house. I laughed so hard I thought I might wet myself; until Da appeared. He fairly raised the roof yelling, "Come you down here wee lad, who in the name of God plays hide and seek on a roof? I'll tell you who, a mental case, and that's you David." Sliding down off the roof, hitching himself to the back door, David leapt to a halt in front of my Da. He was smirking, which made Da madder still. "Get you away home, before I lose my toe in your hole!"

"See you tomorrow, Bill," cried David, running off to his own house.

Da told me to get in the house and out of his sight. Mum said, "Sure it's not his fault, let him have his tea." "Oh, what's the use," muttered Da, as he went upstairs to wash and shave. I can't wait to shave.

I don't like it when they play music and drink in the front room. Mum gets all soppy and wants to hug me and put me on her knee. I'm ten and don't want to sit on her knee, or anybody else's knee.

Tonight is a front room night. Margaret is away to meet her boyfriend. Now that they'll be getting married it's called something else. I don't know what the word is. She says that I can just wear my blazer to the wedding, well, I'm not. I want a proper jacket and a shirt with a tie. No school trousers, no way Jose! I asked if David could come, they all said, 'No,' even Mum.

It's started early in the front room, Da came home on a half day, he wanted to "play in the garden". He doesn't really play, just digs stuff and mows the lawn. Mum was already in her dressing gown and said that he had to go up the hill to the off sales. He looked really fed up.

I don't care, I go upstairs and get my catapult and meet David at the corner, behind the shops. He's got his catapult and a bag of folded paper. "This is the best bit, Bill." He unfolds one of the paper pellets and inside is a tiny stone. "That's brilliant, we can hide here and shoot people," I say.

"We'll have to practice first."

"You're not using me as a target," I tell him. We messed about, hitting trees, tyres and bins. We were ready. Here's Christopher coming, we hated him, a real goody two shoes. He went to the posh school. David wet the pellet, "It'll sting more." He knows quite a lot, he aimed and fired at Christopher, hitting him on the leg. He hopped along clinging to his leg and wailing, "I know it's you two, just wait, just wait….." He couldn't really threaten anything, we stayed down so he couldn't see us. We messed around a bit more and then as it was getting dark we headed home. I didn't want to go home and neither did David, but we'd no money for chips.

We said, "Cheerio," at my gate and I headed round to the back door. Not a sound.

Empty bottles, beer cans and glasses were in the front room. I went back to the kitchen to get something to eat. That's when I saw them; empty pill bottles on the draining board. I charged up the stairs. Da was in bed, snoring his head off and Mum was in the bathroom. What to do, what to do, I charged down stairs and grabbed my blazer, I struggled into it, went out the back and jumped on to my bike. Away I went. Turning the corner I saw Margaret strolling along with her boyfriend. I told her what had happened. "Slow down, slow down, Bill, I can't make out what you're saying. "Mum is in the bathroom, Da is in the bed. There's empty drink bottles, in the front room and pill bottles."

"Empty pill bottles?" she asked.

"Yes, I'm going for Janine." I sped off as they galloped toward the house.

"What are you wearing that blazer over your jeans for? You look like an eejit." Said Janine, when she opened the door of her mate's house.

"Never mind that, Mum's in a bad way. She must have seen that I was nearly crying, "Ok, ok keep your knickers on, 'I've to go home,' she shouted to her mate. She ran alongside me, puffed and not able to ask stupid questions.

We got round the corner and saw the ambulance. Janine sprinted to Margaret, "I'll go in the ambulance with Mum and you stay with Da and our Bill."

"Right, 'phone us when you know anything."

Janine is more street wise than Margaret. More practical, in a way.

Margaret's boyfriend put the kettle on and we sat in the kitchen, not speaking. The 'phone rang, Margaret stood up, but the boyfriend stopped her.

"I'll get it for you."

He came back in and said to Margaret, "You'll have to waken your Da and tell him."

"She's gone?"

He nodded.

If this was a film I'd write in big letters:

THE END

But, it wasn't, not ever.

I needn't worry about blazer or wedding.

Funny the things you think about. Maybe other things are too, too much to think of all at once.

WITHOUT A COAT

Note book in hand she made her way through the front door.

It had been left to her to clear the house, as her two siblings lived too far away.

It had been agreed that she would box what might be kept and dispose of the rest.

The contract had been finally signed and the house needed to be cleared by the end of the month, as this was the twenty seventh this gave her three days. "Crack on, my girl," as her Daddy would have said.

Mum and Dad gone and the money from the house to be divided between them.

Mirror in the hall, how many times had she examined her face in that? Lamenting over spots, plucking eyebrows, reapplying lipstick (Plum julep?) and oh the torture of the false eyelashes.

Wrapping it in bubble wrap, she set it into the packing box and noted it in her book. Two china plates on the wall, bubble wrap and pack. Into the kitchen, thank goodness her Daddy was not one for clutter, this made her job so much easier. Four of everything, spoons, knives, forks, fish slice and tin opener all into the charity box. The cooker, washing machine and 'fridge were spotless and being sold with the house. The cupboard under the sink held her Daddy's shoe cleaning box. She smiled at the memory of him setting their shoes on newspaper and brushing them to a shine. Sunday night, ready for school on Monday morning. Her Brother wanted the box, so he must have fond memories of that ritual too.

Right: into the living room, clock, painting and a brass plaque. Her Aunt had brought that from foreign places. Bubble wrap and into box. Writing furiously in her notebook, she surveyed the room. It was probably 'of its time' but it was so very dated. Not in a good way. Devon grate, side lights, the curtains and carpet threadbare. The new owners had been very kind, assuring her that it would be no trouble to sort out anything left behind. She felt like laughing hysterically when they cooed at her about family home and memories.

Avoiding the sitting room she made her way upstairs. The bathroom was so pokey, and yet as a girl she thought it big. The towels and bed clothes had already been cleared from the hot press, and nothing remained. Into the bedroom she had shared with her Sister. How she had hated being ousted from her own room, to make way for her Brother. Sensing, as always, how she had felt, her Daddy had made her a wardrobe; with a storage box, complete with lock and a key to keep her secret things in. Nothing in here, all gone to the charity shop.

Into her parents' bedroom, only the bedside cabinet remained in here. Tentatively she opened the door, all the legal papers had been removed to the Solicitors office. On the middle shelf remained 'the box.' It was in fact an old biscuit tin, which she now removed and sat on the floor with. It had caused much merriment in the family, she could hear her Daddy's voice clearly," That one's away to the box," her Brother and Sister laughing at her oddity. She didn't mind. Somehow that box had provided comfort then and now. Opening the box she found old familiar items. Faded photographs; her Mother and Father in Dublin, wind-blown and radiant. Daddy, as a young man in Canada, and cycling in Ireland.

Photographs of her younger self and siblings. A three pence piece, her Daddy's union card, an old driving licence and 'a testimonial' as he called it. A reference from previous employers, praising him for his sober ways.

She would keep the old biscuit tin, the others would understand. Into the 'box- room.' Indeed that's exactly what it was. There was nothing left of her Brother or herself in this room.

Back down to the dreaded sitting room.

The hideous piano and furniture were gone.

The memories lingered.

The endless time spent, or so it seemed, of silently waiting on her Daddy to return from the pub.

Seeing the car weaving up the street, the feelings of fear and relief. Fear for the state of him.

In his inebriation she thought of him as 'the different Daddy.' Relief, that the vigil with her Mother was over. As an adult she felt sympathy for her Mother, and could even understand her simmering rage.

Yet, how torturous, for that little girl.

She hoped that the new owners would create happy

memories and a loving, calm atmosphere in this house. Still the words 'sitting room' made her shiver. She slammed the door on that particular memory box.

Making her way through the house, and into the gardens. She surveyed the compost heap, the vegetable garden, the borders of flowers. And in the middle of it all sat the twin swings. One for her, and one for her Sister. She pushed off, soaring higher and higher. Whooping with laughter as she and her Sister had done so many years ago.

Something unlocked inside her and she felt free.

As free as a bird and without shame.

BILL'S STORY

I'm moving to Killiney, but first I've to clean and clear up.

A few scores to settle.

I've bought three houses beside where we used to live. House one, ring the bell, fight the impulse to run away, and wait for someone to answer the door.

"Hello, I don't know if you remember me? I used to live over there," I point in the direction of our old house.

"Let mc think."

He rests his hand on his mouth, brow wrinkled, and snaps his fingers. Twat, always was.

"Oh, yes, you're young Bill, the wee boy whose Mother ……." I cut him off, "Indeed," that's something I learnt from Margaret. When she doesn't want to keep listening she'll stare and say 'indeed'. I'm not giving him the satisfaction of sticking a label on me and putting me back in my box. You need to take another look, haven't worn a blazer in a long time. Don't even like the fancy ones with the brass buttons. No work gear either, no, me 'best bib and tucker', as my Da would have said. Now he's got it. "Won't you come in?" No, I bloody won't. Him and his missus walking past my Mum and Dad in the street, never giving them the time of day. I feel the temper bubble in me, but I fix a smile to my face, "No I won't, thank you, Mr Gad." "Please, please, 'Sean no need to stand on ceremony.'" Yea, but there was a time when you did. "Old habits die hard," I smiled. He knew exactly what I meant.

"The thing is I need to ask you a favour, are you very busy?"

"No, no retired as head of school some time now. Keep up to date, read a lot, generally potter and ponder."

My arse, he's bored and by the looks of the place skint too.

"Well, I've bought a few properties in the district, and was wondering if you could maybe 'potter' in the gardens?"

"Well, I don't know, which gardens would those be?"

"The one next door to you, number fifteen and seventeen."

These gardens were immaculate in all three houses, and he knew it.

"So you would like me to tend the gardens for you?"

Adjust your head, "Well I'll pay you the going rate, of course."

"Glad to oblige," he says, waving his hands.

I want to ask, "Since when?"

"I'll be fair, you can do them when it suits you, and I'll post you a cheque each month."

Of course, he wouldn't be so naff as to ask me how much I'd be paying him. I could see he was bursting to ask, but wouldn't.

"And your poor Father?" God the cheek of him, still wanting to trail me down memory lane. I pretended not to hear. "I'll just bid you goodbye then, Mr Gad."

"I'll get started now, as it's such a nice day," he says.

Yea, go pick a few weeds, if you can find any. It's as near to rubbing your nose in the dirt as I can get. Don't think I'm letting you off that lightly. I've not finished with you yet.

Oh how my Mum would have laughed to think of him gardening for her wee man. Now, on to number nineteen, next to seventeen which I've also bought. Christopher's Mummy, cow of a woman. Telling my Mum that her Son wouldn't amount to anything, unlike her Christopher. Over and over she gloated. Well, let's see who's gloating now. I never liked Christopher, a wimp of a boy, but still I wouldn't want to see him as he is now, living on the streets and begging. She's in the garden, sitting on the summer seat.

I open the gate and walk towards her.

"Oh hello, are you here to service the boiler?" she asks shading her eyes. Needs, her glasses, do I look like someone who services boilers?

"No, Mrs Young, I'm here about Christopher."

"Oh, are you a detective?"

We'll be here all day guessing who I am.

"Maybe, if you put your glasses on, you'll be able to place me."

She reaches for her glasses, I remain standing and look

down at her. Nothing.

"It's me Mrs Young, Bill from number thirteen, do you remember me now?"

Silence, so quiet, I think she's gone to sleep.

"I remember you and that David one, with your pellet guns."

I laughed, "Well that wasn't yesterday. Lovely as it would be to take a walk down memory lane, I'm here with a proposal for you."

"What sort of proposal would you have for me?"

Time to bring you down to earth.

"I saw poor Christopher the other day, I have to say I was shocked. Shame, when you had such high hopes for him."

"Where did you see him?"

So, she hasn't seen him for a while then.

"He was asking strangers for money, I did give him some, but that's not really the answer is it?"

"What are you here for?" she demands sharply. Doesn't want to admit how far down Christopher is.

"I've bought number seventeen and I thought it would be good to give him a roof over his head until I decide to sell the property. I ran the idea past poor Christopher and he was delighted. I thought I'd do the decent thing and run it past you."

Mrs Young was speechless. Oh she had made him a bite to eat, now and again. Christopher said that would only be allowed if it was dark. What trouble would he bring right on her doorstep. All the old neighbours would know, after all her bumming and blowing. It would stick in her craw alright. That upstart Bill owning the house her Christopher was living in. I can just imagine what Christopher will listen to. She realised it was payback time and she was beaten. It had been decided. He'd trash it, of course he would. I had covered that, the buyer was prepared to wait four months. I would have my man in and out in a week to clean and paint it.

"Who'll pay for him to rent it?" she smirked, thinking she'd got me.

"Well, I thought he could be a sort of caretaker, then he wouldn't have to pay any rent at all." Was she going to buy it? Sure her son couldn't care take himself.

"I'll only give him a week's notice when it's to be sold, maybe he could move in with you?"

She spluttered that much, I thought her dentures were going to land at my feet. I wanted to laugh, a great belly laugh, I really did.

A couple of lads firing pellets gave her an excuse to Lord it over my Mum. This was a long time in coming. Poor Christopher, for his Ma, everything was image.

Still, it would give him a good place to stay for a while.

"Well, you're both grown men now, and I know poor Christopher is a bit down on his luck, just at the moment."

Yea, that's one way of putting it.

I'd taken him for a bite to eat, and only I slipped the manager a few pound, we wouldn't have been allowed in. The cut and smell of Christopher was something else. I'd trouble not gagging myself. We'd been ushered to a seat at the back, beside the toilets.

"Well, Mrs Young, he's moving in on Saturday, short flit and all that. I'll give you the key and let Christopher know he's to call with you."

"Two days time, do you say? Sure that's no time, no time at all," she scowled grabbing the key. "Sure I'll have to get everything in order, if my Christopher is to be caretaker for you."

So that's how she was going to play it, her Christopher doing that Bill one a favour. Well, let her see how it felt to have people look down on her, when they saw him walloping up the drive.

"You'll find everything is in tip top order, yes everything in order." She knew exactly what I meant.

Time for the off.

I can hear Mum now, "Oh stop, Bill, Christopher Young living in your house, that's priceless."

I'll never forget the day Mr Lee wrapped our door. It was a bright sunny day. Our Margaret answered the door, "Hello Mr Lee."

"Your father has had a turn in the rhododendron bushes, you need to come and get him NOW." He marched away."

Margaret's face was crimson with humiliation. We had to go to the house and somehow trail him up the street. We never said a word. Mr Lee, Christian pillar of the community, never out of the parish paper. The only good he seemed to do was looking after two rescue dogs. Proof of how caring he was.

This'll be good.

"Good afternoon, I see you still have the dogs." He was sitting in the garden with two old dogs.

"Come in, I can't see you properly."

In I went, sat down on one of his old garden chairs.

"Now, who have we here, young man?"

"I'm Bill, lived up the street."

"I can't recall."

"Well I see your rhododendrons are thriving." Maybe that will refresh your memory, you sanctimonious auld bastard.

I could see him searching his memory. Finally he had it, not a bother to him. Dismissed. Not important.

"Yes I do seem to recall the family." He said this with such disdain that I wanted to punch him.

Instead I smiled.

"Now here's the thing, I do a bit of charity work."

I can imagine Janine squealing at that. "You charity work, don't make me pee my pants." Wait 'till I tell the two sisters, I'll Skype them, so that I can see their faces, when I tell them the whole story.

"That's always a good Christian thing to do, tell me have you found the Lord?"

No, no, we're not going to hide behind the Lord nor the blood of the lamb. He'll be giving me tracts next.

"Mr Lee, the thing is I need your help."

"Well of course, if I can help a fellow man."

Yea right.

"The charity I'm involved with cares for homeless people, young ones."

"God be good" he says, what'll he say when its on his doorstep, well, next door.

"They'll be moving in next door to you, a good Christian influence I thought. Anyway they have a few dogs, give them something to love and care for. The dogs will be outside, but fenced in. The young people don't know how to, well clean up after them?"

"You can't do that, it must be against the law," he spluttered. I could see him trying to process the information. This young upstart Bill was asking him to shovel shit. No, that couldn't be right.

I've bought the house on a buy to let basis, Mr Lee, and it is not against the law to rent it out to three young people who are in reduced circumstances. The fact that they happen to have well behaved rottweilers each, to keep them safe on the streets or here is not an issue." Put that in your pipe.

"Reduced circumstances, issue?" I must have been listening to Margaret more than I thought.

"So you want me to help them clean up after the dogs, is that it?"

Here it comes, how he'd love to help but, blah, blah, blah.

Only a fool would agree to this.

"The thing is, the Parish magazine are doing a feature on this, quite an article, double page spread. Integration into the community. I thought it would be grand if you could feature in it?"

"Oh, yes?" he asked puffing himself up.

"A respected Christian neighbour who's lending support, don't you think?"

How many palms did I have to grease to make this happen?

Those dogs would bite the arms of you. He'd have his work cut out for him cleaning after them. The Parish paper were sending someone to write the article and I had organised a photographer in six weeks time. He couldn't afford to let the doggy poo build up. What alternative did he have? Win, win.

"Eh, what am I to do with the eh, excrement?"

"Well, that's easy peasy, the council have agreed to put in a few wee bins, just dump it in there, I'll leave you some poop bags. So that's sorted."

"I haven't agreed to anything, yet," he grumbled.

Time to spell it out, I smiled broadly at him.

"Well, if you don't want to do it, that's okay, really it is, the only thing is I need to make the Parish magazine aware of any obstructions I've met with along the way, comprendi?"

That would be the end of your holier than thou image.

If you were a man at all, you'd knock me on my back and tell me where to get off.

"I'll help, yes, I'll do my Christian duty, when did you say they're moving in?"

I didn't, they're fly these auld ones.

"Oh, they'll be here in a day or two, not sure exactly when."

Not enough time for him to dream up any mischief.

Three months he'd have to suffer.

I bid him farewell and if I had had a hat I'd have doffed it at him.

Mr Lee shovelling shit, who'd have thought it?

Maybe he could spread it round his rhododendrons?

I wish David was here, he would totally 'get' what I had done. We could sit at the back of the shops, share a bottle of Strongbow, and piss ourselves laughing. I miss my old mate. He should never have got into the 'hard' stuff. Passed a good few years back.

Now the final house.

Back to Mr Gad.

Didn't think he was getting away with a few weeds, did you? No siree.

It's beginning to get dark.

Pity, I'd love to see his face.

I go into the house next door to him. I put the porch light

on, not exactly red, but not far off it.

Oh brilliant his light has come on, the nosey bugger is coming out.

"Oh, Bill, I thought I heard something, and thought I'd come out to check. Can't be too careful."

You ain't seen nothin' yet.

Flip, who am I?

I sound like rootin' tootin' cowboy Bill.

Just a bit of kindness to me and mine would have meant a great deal. Don't they realise I'm still that boy in a man's clothes with money and a fancy car? I feel as if I want to cry, no, howl.

Just in time, a taxi pulls up and out steps 'Irma'.

She's a working girl and I have a lot of time for her (and no, I haven't sampled the goods).

'Irma' is her working name, and that's how I refer to her.

Anyway, she's wearing a purple sparkly thing. It just about 'covers her modesty', as my Da would have said. Her long legs tanned and gorgeous; wearing more bling than a Christmas tree.

Mr Gad stepped forward.

Irma vaulted the gate, "Hello, there, sweetie pie," she growled pulling him to her ample bosom.

"My goodness, Mr Gad, will I leave you two to get better acquainted?"

Who is so uppity now?

He was speechless, spluttering, puffing and purple in the face, I thought Irma had overdone her instructions a bit.

Irma, come lets get you settled.

"Sure, bye now, sweetie, I'm sure we'll be seeing plenty of each other.

She batted her false eyelashes, vaulted the gate again, this time giving him an eyeful of her arse.

Mr Gad backed into his house and shut the door.

Three to four months of torture and mayhem.

Serve them right.

Sorted.

JANINE'S STORY

Nearly seven months she took to clear out Da's house. I was raging with her. It was alright for Bill, he didn't need the money, but I did. I said nothing, well, I did ask a few times. It was always the same, "I'm not ready yet." I couldn't say what I really wanted to, "When will you be bloody ready?" but, I couldn't. I was over here by then and after the hack of her at Da's funeral, well, to tell you the truth I was scared to.

We all sort of went our separate ways after Mum died. Margaret and I tried our best for Da and Bill. It wasn't easy, but, I'm not going over all that again. Anyway, Da died years after Mum. Margaret was on her own, that useless man she took up with was gone. I asked Bill about him and he said, "Margaret's lost the plot over him." Nobody who knew her could believe it. His kids from previous relationships, he didn't work, wasn't a looker, he gambled and he was a chaser. Eventually it fell to bits. I don't know the whole story, just bits and pieces. I think she was ashamed and didn't want to talk about it, even Da thought she was on drugs.

Da and her were always thick as thieves, even more so when he got sober. She organised everything to do with the funeral. A soloist sang a few songs, ones my Da liked and a hymn 'abide with me.' Margaret looked well in a lovely black suit, thank God she'd ordinary wee shoes on. She spoke from the heart about Da, and there wasn't a dry eye in the house. As funerals go, it was fine. The 'refreshments' as she called them were tea, coffee or a soft drink. A nice spread but no alcohol. I said nothing, I knew she was strung out.

Just the family went to the grave. That's when she lost it. Standing rigid as a statue, and wearing this long tatty coat that was far too big for her. A bit odd, with all that finery underneath. I couldn't see her hands the cuffs were that long.

Click.

Jasus.

She was wearing Da's dexter.

Oh oh.

She opened her mouth and screamed to the skies.

Bill and I went to comfort her, just kept sobbing over and over. "My Daddy is dead." Well, he was our Da too, you'd a thought she was about four. What with the big coat and her making a show of herself.

Anyway that was then and this is now.

I've been over in England a long time. I moved away. I couldn't stand the memories, nor the man I married. Me and the three kids, well they're not kids anymore. I live on the outskirts of – oops nearly said it. I won't say anymore, even after all this time I'd be afraid he'd land over.

I rent a lovely wee place and I've a few good mates. We go to the 'women's institute', yea, that's right me at that. It's not all twin set and pearls. I don't have any. I've been developing the arts and crafts. Well, mostly the crafts, but I do go to a wee art class. Two of the women cook something to share and teach us how to make it. Many a time in the past they had somehow managed to make too much. Accidentally on purpose, I'd say. I had to take it home or it would go to waste. The kids were delighted. We support and inspire each other. It's not just about cooking, craft and flower arranging. It's fund-raising, competitions, educating and we have a good laugh. I feel as if I belong. We offer practical help; transport to important appointments, decorating a room, and gardening. Never does money cross hands, we just know if we need we get. Not in a big showy way, just quietly and the best we can. Margaret said that it was really brave of me to move. I don't know about that, but I do know that if I'd stayed I would have ended up in a psychiatric ward or dead. That's not me exaggerating either.

I have rented a wee shop too, and that's how I make my living. I always liked crafts and it still amazes me what people will pay for upcycled stuff. I buy old bits and bobs. Change handles and clean, sand and paint. I gather up old plates, lights, boxes, anything as long as it has something about it. I don't know what that something is, I just know it when I see it. A bit of elbow grease and then I see what I can do. I even have a few regulars who will put in an order.

My latest is an old nursing chair, oh it's lovely. I sanded it down and painted it a lovely lilac colour. I don't buy expensive chalk paint, I just add a bit of chalk to the paint. I stuck sparkly navy stars on the back of it and varnished the whole thing. I decided it needed something else so I knit a cushion in lilac, purple and navy.

Mum taught me to knit, I took to it. What a laugh, Margaret tried to knit a waistcoat. It would have fitted a small family. She must have spent a fortune on wool never mind the 'phone calls to me. Couldn't understand the pattern. It was as if we'd joined a secret club and plotted to make a simple task complicated, excluding her, of course. Anyway, as usual I'm away somewhere else.

I have a wee blue van, it's old but reliable. I love it, everyone calls it 'Janny's blue bird' and as I tootle past, I'm recognised and people wave at me. Do you want to know what my wee house is like?

Well, maybe you do and maybe you don't. Indulge me, I'm that proud I could burst, so you see, I have to tell you.

I have two big grey pots on either side of the yellow door. There's a parking space at the front. Straight into the living room and kitchen. It's all painted a neutral colour. Think of the colour of cord for wrapping parcels, well, that's the colour. There's an upcycled cabinet in the corner. It's so bright, I don't think I need any other colour, except for a few cushions I made. I made a throw out of a tartan remnant. It sits folded over the arm of the neutral sofa. Cosy around my legs in colder weather. The kitchen is off the living room and again it's the same neutral colours. But with duck egg appliances and worktops. I look out onto a wooded area and can watch the squirrels overhead. There's a tiny back patio and I have an old metal table and a few chairs. All painted in random colours. It's a wee haven and a sun trap in the summer. The bathroom is black and white, and I change the towels when I feel like it. Sometimes pink, sometimes red and then there's my favourite duck egg blue.

There are just two bedrooms, it was more than a bit cramped when the kids were younger, but we muddled through. The two eldest have flown the nest, so, it's just me and the youngest. We have a bedroom each, bliss. Mine is a bit girly, all pink and twinkly lights. The other is a bit of a tip, but, it's not my bedroom. It'll be empty soon enough, and I can do it up whatever way I want. I give it a good tidy when Margaret comes over. Yes, she comes over about four times a year, for short visits. No point in tempting fate.

I remember the first time she came over, you could still see the grief of not having Da. I suppose too, whatever she had been through with the waste of space. I was shocked. Our Margaret like an old shuffling woman. I didn't say anything, but let me tell you it wasn't a basket of laughs. I sort of nursed her a bit. I took her to the WI and for once she took a back seat. The women sensed she was frail and they showered her with kindness. On the short walk home, we linked arms and she said to me, "You've found your ladies then" a statement, it took me a minute or two to realise what she was talking about, "I'd forgotten that, remember I used to talk through the hedge to the woman who lived behind us?" "Yes, that's what I meant, you were always chatting to old ladies," says Margaret. "My ladies aren't old," I say, a bit sharpish.

"No, but that's what you called them then too"

"What?" I ask her.

"My ladies," she replies.

She's right, I did.

"What was that all about?"

"Do you think I'm going to counsel you and then get an ear bashing for my troubles?"

We both laugh and know that's exactly what would happen.

Back in the house and she flops onto the sofa, she lifts a cushion, examining it.

"That's not the material from the swing cost is it?"

"The very same," I reply.

"Oh, I'm so pleased."

She's a bit daft like that, sentimental, kept Da's old tin box.

I won't be mentioning that, she'll think I'm spoiling for a fight, and she'd be gurning over Da.

"The place is lovely Janine. It really is, I like what you've done to it."

"Thanks," I said, I knew she meant it.

"Drink your tea, and then away to bed."

"I don't like tea," she said.

"I know you don't but you're not getting coffee to keep you awake and me with you."

Meekly she went to bed. I slipped a jar in to warm the bed for her. She'll probably be blubbering about that too.

I can see that she's not tough and strong, our Margaret's just as vulnerable as most. By the time she was ready to go back and return to work, I thought she looked a good bit better. The roles have blended over the years, still she managed to boss me a bit, always a good sign with her, the thing is I don't mind so much, not now when time is so short. The difference is I boss her too and both of us are doing it for the good of the other. Well, so we say.

Now that visit was for a week, four days would be enough. Slowly we'll work it out. I don't think she will want to stay for a full week. I don't go back at all, and she doesn't ask me anymore. There's nothing for me. The kids are within driving distance of me. Their friends and work are all over here.

The last time Margaret came it was really a good visit and we laughed so much, well I nearly peed my pants. Margaret sort of squeals and cries when she's laughing. She was hugging the checked cushion, and the tears were tripping her. There are lots of memories only we share and I suppose Bill a bit too.

Here's what happened:

Before Margaret came to visit me, Bill contacted her and said we'd to wait for him to Skype us on the Sunday night. Margaret was leaving on Monday. Four days. Grand.

Margaret says "We've to have lots of tissues and popcorn".

"I hope it's not bad news?" asks Margaret. I used to think she was being a smart arse, well, sometimes she is. Mostly, though she's trying to work something out. Like the time she asked the wee girl in the hotel, "Why would I want to eat my dinner of a slate?"

I felt like crawling under the table, the wee girl says, "Would you like me to put your dinner on a plate?"

"Yes I would thank you, but I don't understand why it came on a slate?"

The wee girl says, "I don't know" and lifts her slate.

Now before we get into asking the management to explain to her, I say, "I'm grand with mine as it is." When the girl leaves she says to me, "Janine, are you sure you're happy to eat your dinner of a slate?"

"Yes, I'm grand, its a fad, Margaret, a trendy thing."

"Yes, but ..."

"Leave it with the slate, Margaret."

See what I mean? She's like somebody with tourettes.

I remember the time she said to Mum, "You said I was

premature?"

Mum got all bristly, "Yes, that's right"

"Well, how come I was nearly ten pounds?" I was too young to understand, of course I do now. The only thing I knew then was that I was delighted when she got a wack round the ear!

I'm away again, back to popcorn night.

I've moved the computer onto a table and brought it up close.

We have the blanket over us both and we're waiting.

Bill comes up on the screen. I haven't seen him for a while. He's getting old too.

"Hello, all sitting comfortably I see, now before we begin I want to introduce you to someone."

The screen fills with this woman, waving like mad, "Hello girls, I'm Irma", then she's away. I don't get it. I mean she's gorgeous and all that, but she's clearly, as my granny would have said, "A street walker".

I don't understand, Bill why are you introducing us to this woman?" asks Margaret.

"Never mind now, it'll be clear soon enough, so don't

bother trying to work anything out Margaret," says Bill.

We both sit back, I concentrate, and try to put the image of 'Irma' out of my head. He tells us he's bought three properties beside where we used to live. Big deal, he's always buying places. He says one of them is Gad's house, and he's got him gardening at the other two. Margaret and I snigger at that, imagine that stuck up old goat gardening for Bill.

He then moves on to poor Christopher. Well, it's so long ago, all I remember is a spoilt boy and Mum coming in after meeting his Mum and raving about her wee man out shining that brat of a boy. I couldn't believe what Bill had done and Christopher a druggie. Sure there'd be all sorts of comings and goings at that house. Margaret and I look at each other dumbfounded.

"Remember the Lee's?"

Margaret blushes to the roots of her hair.

"I see you do Margaret, what about you?" he asks me.

"The stuck up ones, he was all churchy, thought we were dirt, them?"

"Yep, not so stuck up now, I have him shovelling shite."

When he told us the story of Mr Lee we had to tell him to

stop for a minute, we were laughing that much. Margaret and I were clutching each other, the tears rolling down our faces.

"I'm away to get a cup of tea, I'll be back in five minutes, give you two time to compose yourselves." Bill disappears from the screen.

I have to go to the toilet or I swear I'll wet myself.

Margaret is clutching her side and gasping between laughs, "Hurry up, I need to go too."

We settle back down. God, this is great, better than a film.

He's back.

"Right, enough with the merriment, remember Irma?" he asks.

We both nod at the screen

He's started laughing now too, big deep haw haw haw's, we wait patiently. No wonder he is laughing. I can just picture that big girl hoisting her dress up, not that there was much to begin with. Her arse in Mr Gad's face.

Margaret has composed herself, well enough to ask,

"How long will these tenants be staying, Bill?"

"About three months, it's all sorted. Enough for them to know what has happened to each other and why. Although I'd say they've a good enough idea anyway."

"Nite, God bless and mind the roads," that's what Mum always said to him. With a wave of his hand, he's gone. He did all this for Mum and I suppose for Da and Margaret and me.

We would get a lot of mileage out of this.

Margaret and I talked about it all late into the night.

I even allowed her a cup of that strong coffee she drinks.

I reckoned the two of us were that hyped up that it didn't matter.

I asked her, "How come you blushed so much when Bill mentioned the Lee's?"

"I still remember it as though it were yesterday. Daddy had a turn in the rhododendron bushes, it wasn't his finest hour", poor Margaret, loyal to the end.

We looked at each other and cracked up again.

It was just so prim of her. We both knew what 'a turn' meant. Da legless and shouting the odds. The shame of it too, her and Bill trying to get him home in broad daylight.

I bet they never gave us a thought. Horrible they were, so when Margaret says, "Do you think Bill is a bit, well, severe on them, Janine?" I feel like smacking her, hard.

I say instead, "Don't you like the idea of Mr all that's holy, shovelling shite?"

"Yes, but …."

I cut her off.

"No buts, Margaret, they deserve every bit of it. It's only until the houses are sold. We were just children, and they showed us no kindness at all, in fact they rubbed our noses in it."

"You're right of course you are. Wasn't that 'Irma' gorgeous?" she asks.

"Yea, wonder if the old boy will be greasing her hand?"

"What with?" asks Margaret, then realising what she's said, we're off again.

By the time we got to bed, we were both sore with laughing.

Time marches on for us all. We don't begin to imagine it when we're young and fresh or what we carry with us.

I have my times of light and shadow.

Must tell Margaret that, she'll appreciate the turn of phrase.

Nite, nite all.

Your Shame My Shame

Wits' End

Jacqueline McClenaghan

THE WIDOWER

I'm Margaret's father, proud of her, in my own way. I'm not demonstrative, that's not my way. I'm a widower, used now to being on my own. I don't only love Margaret, but, I like her too. We share the same sense of dry humour; we're a bit stubborn, independent and hard-working. Margaret had three jobs on the go to get her through University. I was at the graduation, proud as a peacock, I said to her, "You clean up well", she knew what I meant, that I was proud of her, some things don't need to be said, you just feel them. Now, she wouldn't agree with me, but, she's a naïve girl and that has always been her downfall.

Married, when she was only twenty, a doctor, if you please. It didn't work out, I don't know why. I said to her, "He seems like a right fellow." "You don't have to live with him" she said. Well, that didn't invite further discussion now, did it?

I know most of her friends, most of them she's known a long time. Right wee girls they are. Listen to me calling them 'wee girls' but, that's what they are to me, even if they are in their forties.

I do what I can to help her, wee jobs about her house and garden. The clutter of her would give you a sore head.

We've some great chats and laughs and if she wasn't my daughter, well, I'd like her anyway.

She told me that she'd never marry again, just said, "It doesn't suit me." Oh she's had boys over the years, but, nothing serious, said that they were "heavy maintenance".

I was surprised when she 'phoned and told me that she was bringing someone with her to visit me. "Don't worry about tea, I'll get fish and chips for us on the way over," she said.

"No vinegar for me," I told her.

"Well duh, I know that. We'll be there about half past six," she said.

As usual she bounced in through the back door, but

what wasn't usual was the crater she brought with her. What was I supposed to say, "Pleased to meet you?" Well, I wasn't, and neither would you, if you'd seen the cut of him. I managed a nod and a "How to do." I looked at my daughter, and knew that she felt my immediate dislike. There'd be a chat about that later alright.

Where to start? I've worked all my days and I can tell you that boy was a stranger to hard work. To quote Margaret he had 'heavy maintenance' written all over him.

Margaret set out the fish and chips, well, they'd hardly hit the plates when he was shovelling them into him as if someone was about to steal his plate. The talk of him too, well, I've worked with men from all parts, different accents, and different ways of speaking, so I'm no snob. This 'George' chattered away like a chimp.

I couldn't believe she could bear to listen to him. Well listen she did, with a big soft look on her face. The same look she had when I bought a wee dog for her, now, what was its name? 'Bambi', that was it, the name of the dog. I wondered had she started taking drugs. I'd read about that, sensible people going off the rails. There was something up; this wasn't like her, not like her at all. Smitten, that's what she was.

I finished my tea and then said, "I'm just going into the garden," even though it was drizzling, I had to escape. There was to be no escaping George. Didn't he follow me out, feckless he was, didn't know a dahlia from a dandelion. Chatter, chatter; about pubs and bookies, auld nonsense talk.

I grunted a few times, thought that would shut him up. Like heck it did, next thing he's 'confiding' in me about his 'great feelings' for Margaret. 'Not appropriate' she would have said, if she was at herself and heard him. Me? Well, I'm not a violent man, but, I felt like burying my spade in his thick skull. I mean, I've just met him, and he's talking in this way that I wouldn't have, well I wouldn't have with anybody. The sweat was breaking on me; I had the 'jitters'.

Thank God, Margaret called us in for tea.

Four buns he ate, leaving one each for Margaret and me. About half past eight Margaret says, "We'd better go, George has to be back at the hostel for nine."

Hostel? Did she say 'hostel'? Maybe she said 'hotel'.

"Did you say 'hostel' Margaret?" I asked her.

"Yes, that's right Dad." No explanation, well that'd come later, my girl. This was bad, very bad indeed!

I made a great show of washing my hands at the sink, so that I wouldn't have to shake hands with him. "My granny always washed at the 'jaw box'" says George and Margaret laughing like a drain.

Dear God, sure, nobody says 'jaw box' any more.

"Bye Dad, I'll call in on Thursday, I've some time due to me so I'll be here about four."

"Will I be coming too Mags?" asks George. 'Mags', what's that all about?

"No, no, George, it'll just be a quick visit."

"Sure, I could help your Dad in the garden again."

I snorted, I couldn't help it.

Margaret glared at me, "See you on Thursday."

Yes you will indeed Madam, I thought.

I hope he's not with her.

HER STORY

Margaret parked her car and painfully made her way to the cafe where she would meet Peter. It must be thirty years since she had last seen him, escorted to the waiting van, which would take him, yet again, to the prison where he would serve time for his pathetic petty crimes. George at her side, sullen and defeated, losing hope that his oldest son would somehow, redeem and reform himself. She shook herself and stopped at a bistro, which, was more to her liking than the greasy spoon which Peter had named through the solicitor. The coffee arrived and she allowed herself to reflect on the strange telephone call several nights ago.

"This is 'Mac and Mac' solicitors may I speak with Margaret Heath?"

Why did they all have these double names, was it an

affectation? Where there two 'Mac's? Margaret trailed her meandering thoughts back to the telephone. She must stop this, well, maybe reign it in a bit.

"Yes, speaking."

"Well Ms Heath, or may I call you 'Mag's?"

No one called her that ever and she did not want this stranger to address her in a familiar fashion which made her ache.

"If you don't mind, I prefer Ms Heath."

Who cared if he minded, she minded. Don't be such a sissy Margaret.

"Very well Ms Heath I am acting on behalf of Peter Alison, well, really, his father George, with whom I believe you were once acquainted?"

Dear heavens, 'once acquainted' what inadequate jargon for someone who impacted so thoroughly on her mind, her spirit and her body for years.

"Yes," she whispered.

"Well the thing is, his son, would like to meet you and entrust you with a key, which you will undertake to return to me. I have supplied him with a large stamped addressed envelope, of course, he may lose it, but, could I request that you ensure it is returned?"

"You could, and I will."

Some things never changed, a forty eight year old man who couldn't mind an envelope.

Margaret wanted to refuse, but, curiosity got the better of her, as, of course, George was counting on, and so she agreed.

At sixty-five Margaret had a bit of trouble with her mobility and would have said, had she been asked, that, 'the winters have not been kind to me'. In this she would have been wrong. A handsome woman, a face hinting at intelligence and humour. A style which, without any guile she had made her own. Today she was wearing black jeans, DMs and a scarlet jumper, a cream cashmere wrap around her shoulders and a soft cream suede bag across her body. He was sitting outside, looking exactly what he was, a feral faced recidivist.

"Hello Margaret, I'd have known you anywhere."

She nodded and sat down.

He eyed her carefully, sussing if there was anything in this meeting for him. Margaret wished she had possessed the savvy to accurately assess these takers years ago. She toyed with the idea of stringing him along, revenge?

No, she had outgrown that particular little game of spite.

"Right, Peter, let's cut to the chase, what's this about?"

Sulky look, playing with his tea, his roll ups, matches, finally.

"Do you want something to drink?"

Yea right and maybe an 'all day big breakfast' for you, which I'll be mug enough to pay for. Me thinks not.

"No thank you."

Silence – well she could do silence too.

Finally, when he realised she was not biting, he gave her the information.

"My Da is in intensive care, he gave me the key and said for you to visit the house, you know?"

"Yes, I know, not senile yet."

"You're to send the key back to yer man, you know?"

There was no reason to affirm that she did know, she had forgotten how he habitually and annoyingly ended every sentence with 'you know?'

"Why am I to visit the house? Straight, simple, no sarcasm."

"He said you'd know, you know?"

Oh yessy. Indeed she did, he wanted somehow for her to feel what had overwhelmed them both all those years ago.

"Anyway, it's like he's not expected to last and you've to see the house before he snuffs it, you know?"

He said this importantly, not even aware of how gross and offensive he was.

"Yes before you can sell it and get your hands on the money", thought Margaret. It gave her no satisfaction to be right about this odious creature or his grasping siblings, and she couldn't bear to be in his presence a moment longer.

"Right then, I will visit the house and return the key to the solicitor."

"Oh, shit, I think I left the envelope in the hostel. Margaret, you couldn't see your way to, you know?"

Anything she would have given him would have been too little, and she would have been the subject of how smart he was to con her out of whatever. Let him dream up some other entertaining little story, with him the big guy to some unsuspecting silly sap. 'Not I, said Little Red Hen,' thought Margaret.

"I'll do as your father requested, goodbye."

Margaret made her way back to the car, he would tell George she was going, she had given nothing else to tell him, no messages to pass on or be twisted in the telling. He would know in her action that she was telling him that she still cared and was finally letting him go. Margaret hoped with all her being it would bring him a little peace.

Curiosity and anticipation were getting the better of her and she could delay no longer. Two days later off she went.

With a simple picnic in the boot of her car, her tote and a big woolly coat, she set off, estimating a fifty minute journey which would take her back to the once familiar streets.

This was a bit spooky, propelling her into her past as though time had not moved on.

The area had changed little, a bit more 'gentrified' she supposed.

Margaret pulled up outside the house and took the key from her pocket. She held it lovingly in her hand and wondered if it was his original key. Had he ever been back? Somehow she doubted it. Since he had moved out and on he would not inflict the memories that returning would bring.

The little plaque was still screwed to the wall, 'Wits End' some joker had painted a 'T' in front of it. She smiled at this.

The front garden was unkempt and tangled weeds stood waist high, empty cans and food wrappers, amongst them, like a horrible dump. This offended her and she had to make herself turn the key quickly in the lock.

Closed up, it retained a vague smell which she instantly recognised; a musky after shave and tobacco. Walking straight through to the kitchen she put her bag on the floor, leaning her arms on the sink and looking out of the back window. There was an old plastic chair, but, in her memory she visualised the table and chairs, where they had breakfasted on fresh fruit salad and yogurt. The statue they had found on a skip and laughingly named 'Bertha'. Maybe she would picnic out there later. Turning away from the window she noticed something shiny on the counter.

'Counter' that was his word for work top, she had thought it spontaneously. It was the 'zippo' lighter she had brought him back from her only holiday without him. Left behind and forgotten. She left the kitchen and went into the small sitting room – 'parlour' she heard him say in her head. Meals had been eaten there, but, mostly they held no powerful memories. Into the hall, and up the stairs. On the return she went into 'their' bedroom. She laughed aloud as her eyes caught the centre light shade. He had said it looked like 'Tommy Cooper's' hat. It did.

On to the front bedroom. Remembering, how, before the wardrobes came, she had returned home to find that he had randomly hammered nails into the walls and hung her clothes on them. "You can have your own wee shop." She bit back the hysteria, even now, remembering how she knew not to mention the damage to the plaster or the thousands squandered at the bookies, which could have bought enough wardrobes to furnish the whole area, never mind this bedroom. Keep it real, she thought, okay, a little sentimentality but the days of pretending are long, long, gone. Margaret made her way into the bathroom which was as she remembered it. Black and white tiled floor, big old fashioned sink and a huge deep bath. His meanness had paid off for here was a treasure of 30's chic. She looked at the bath and remembered all the nights she had escaped, locking the door and immersing in a warm comforting scented bath. Stilling her mind and body for the night ahead and whatever it might bring.

Margaret made her way to the kitchen and felt emotionally wrung out. She lifted her bag and turning the key she carefully descended the steps, covered in algae, that's all she would need to slip and fall here. Out into the garden.

Although it was quite warm for early May, she was glad of the protection her woolly coat gave her, as she perched on the back step. The plastic chair lay in the midst of the nettles and she didn't feel up to negotiating that tangle. Opening her bag she set out her picnic. Coffee, a cheese sandwich and a small bar of chocolate.

Pouring the coffee from her flask, she closed her eyes, took a sip and allowed herself to indulge, one last time on the journey with George which consumed her all those years ago. She felt she owed it to them both.

Margaret knew from the time she connected with him that she would leave him. Didn't she?

The odds were against any form of succession, weren't

they? Was it inevitable or had they created the whole sorry saga?

Margaret was the tutor – he the pupil. Nothing dodgy, you understand, an adult rehabilitation group for supposedly recovering alcoholics. "So not my type, small tattooed and a series of drink related wounds," she would have said, had she been asked. Not a package that indicated balance and sorted. Maybe it was the keenness of his intellect, the cynical humour. Maybe it was something more basic, the broad shoulders, the big eyes, or the bad boy attitude. Who knows? Maybe something more deeply psychological. Dynamics reminiscent of her mother and father, grandfather, perhaps? How far back to go in this analysis? Does any of it matter now?

Only the ever present mental pain and legacy.

He hovered around for a long time. Always in the kitchen after the group had ended. In the car, claiming his space beside her. Managing to sit next to her in the 'bonding' group at the cafes. The long meaningful looks, showing he 'got it' when the others did not understand something. So, the link was established. When the group ended he came back. To get his work folder. Right. He had as much interest in a work folder as she had in cake decoration. Nil. He hung about until she was leaving. "Could you give me a lift, please?" "Where are you going?" she asked. "Just into town." As they approached the city centre, she asked "OK, George where will it be?" Apparently, he was having a solitary tea before retiring to the hostel for the night. What could she do? Yes, yes, with hindsight drop him off and accelerate. Hard. Did she? No.

Dining in a down market restaurant in Ballynahinch, they talked endlessly, laughed slightly manically and she began to bestow qualities on him, which, his own mother would have had trouble recognising. Painting a picture by numbers and making him fit the picture. She advised him that the last bus was about to go, but, he looked so terribly hurt and rejected that she offered him the spare room in her house. What the hell was she thinking? She wasn't. Loneliness, boredom, company, an adventure, excitement – all of these – none of these. There was certainly a void, whatever the reasoning, and he was about to fill it. Fill it? If only she had known, he filled It ; over flowed it. He played her like a violin. They arrived at her home, had tea and coffee and drove into Newcastle. They walked, not touching, along the promenade. It rained, heavily. "We're soaked to the skin," he said. She found his Belfast accent, pronunciation, and colloquialisms entertaining. He had a host of them:

chaclate (chocolate)

huspital (hospital)

beg (bag)

flawers (flowers).

He made no apologies, and marvelled at her wonderment.

Back at the ranch, he was ensconced in the spare room. Not for long, he wandered into her room and into her bed. "Move over," he said. She laughed nervously, for she knew that this would be the point of no return. The fire that would not be extinguished. Whatever.

The next day there was a meeting of funders on the outskirts of Belfast and Margaret was getting ready to go.

"I'll come with you to the wee meetin'" said George.

"Bugger off," she said internally.

Outwardly, "Sure it'll be really boring, I'll meet up with you afterwards."

With hindsight (isn't that a great wisdom to have after turmoil and pain?) she was setting the picture to placate this man/child.

"I've left me wallet in your place."

"I'll lend you ten pounds."

No 'thank-you' and the money was never paid back. Sure, why make a fuss about something so trivial?

Warning bells a-plenty. She didn't make a choice to ignore them, only to put them away, far away in a box on a different shore. Did she think she could 'fix' him? Maybe. How arrogant and misguided.

So began a pattern of sorts.

"Wouldn't you like to get out of the hostel?"

"Yea, I will."

"Have you put your name down for a flat?"

"Don't worry, it'll happen."

"You could own your own house, go to college, you're clever enough."

"Don't be daft."

Margaret was relentless and George began to bask in her belief of him and his abilities.

Margaret was going to France for a week, a holiday

which had been arranged before this had begun.

Before she left, a one bedroom flat had been secured. Oh, the joy of it, they sat outside gazing up at this wee place. Confident of the happiness it would bring them. A place of his own, indeed. She oscillated between pity (he had nothing) and joy (playing house). He didn't know how he would manage and promised her that he would have it lovely for her coming back. The relationship was two months old and in the magical insane phase. Very intense, long talks, debates, the walks, the 'flawers', the cinema, dinners in and out. He came to her house and stayed for days at a time. She cooked and catered like a dervish. Of course, they couldn't keep their hands off each other. The sixty-five year old Margaret smiled at this memory. Where did all that heady (toxic) stuff go to?

The more she tried, the more he denied. She put his insulting ignorance down to his troubled past, upbringing, not working, lack of structure. Oh, yes she had plenty of excuses for him. There were not many compliments, few appreciations and the insidious put downs. She could not understand – one minute it was breakfast in bed and the next it was: "Why de ye have to take so long to get ready, it doesn't make you look any better." Margaret would be so appalled and stunned that she would laugh at his audacity. This resulted in him stomping off, muttering as he went. Funny, if you're an infant. She saw nothing more harmful in this than a 'boy' having a strop. Yes, yes, that old friend hindsight. Margaret went to France with her friend 'Josie'. They had been friends since University, and remained kindred spirits. They did the tourist trail in Paris, and travelled on to a small port called 'Cairn Carneou'. The holiday was peaceful and relaxing. Cafes, reading and watching the world go by.

Margaret talked to Josie about George.

"I can't believe you are so smitten with someone so, well, opposite," said Josie. "I'm glad for you, although I have to say he does sound like hard work." Cautious words of warning from a good friend.

Heady stuff for a woman who had been on her own for a long time.

Margaret and Josie went shopping. "What are you buying for Mr Wonderful?" Josie asked, laughing good naturedly at her friend, who was, as usual trying to get it just right. She bought him a lovely lighter, some French cigars, silly fridge magnets and a tourist map of France.

She couldn't wait now that it was the last day to get back to him. See what he'd done to the flat and make sure that this wasn't a silly infatuation.

Arriving home there were four messages from him on the answer machine.

She unpacked, made a few calls and perched beside the 'phone so that when he called she was ready gifts in hand to head out the door and drive up the road to George. They hugged and then became a bit shy and uncertain of each other.

He'd bought a second hand suite of furniture – mink brown velour. Yuck. She hated it. She dutifully admired it. He examined his gifts, "That's grand." No 'thank you'. "Well, what's the news?" she chirped gaily.

He proudly informed her that he'd been to the college and had been accepted on the course which would allow him entry to university. "That's brilliant, well done you, when do you start?" she asked. "The beginning of September. You'll give us a hand won't you?" "Yes, yes, but you know I'll be working." "I'm only asking for a bit of a hand, just till I find me feet and get into the way of it." Margaret dreaded to think what 'a bit of a hand' meant.

"Yes, and I've said I'll help, but, I will be working."

"Maybe I shouldn't bother then."

"No, now don't be like that, I will help."

He glared at her, hurt and wounded, that she would not assure him that he would get one hundred percent support. She could feel an atmosphere coming on. In order to diffuse the situation she suggested they go and get some food. It seemed the purchase of the grotty suite was about all he had managed to add to the flat.

She had asked him previously not to smoke in the car, but, as soon as they got in he lit up. She reminded him, "George, I'd really rather you didn't smoke in the car." He laughed, and mimicked her, "I'd really rather, oh you're a real Bunty, sure the windee's down what harm is there?" The shopping in the supermarket was a nightmare. Him tossing in buns, cake, lemonade and sweets, her explaining why she chose olives, cheese, pannini's and where she acquired the taste for filter coffee. By the time they were loading the car, she was irritated, confused and deflated. This was not the romantic home coming she had envisaged. She felt her good will and energy seeping away. "Why so sad Mags?" His pet name for her brought a smile, "Just a bit tired, I suppose."

"Well then how's about an early night?"

"Yes please." And so it was, until the next episode.

The next day he was up and about at eight, he explained that this was a left over from the boys' home. She didn't respond, not wanting to hear any more sad boy tales. He insisted that she get up, so as not to "waste the day".

"Well, okay then, ten at the latest, we can go into town and I can do a wee bet."

Great. Can't wait. She got up, showered and dressed and off they went, walking into town. They got as far as the junction of Bedford Street, when he broke into a jog, she quickly followed. It rapidly ceased to have any amusement, if it ever had. She followed behind and when she reached the cafe in Botanic he was already seated and served. Tea for one. She ordered coffee. "What was all that about?" she asked. He shrugged his shoulders.

"Tell you what, I'll finish this and make my way to the flat. I'll get the car and go home."

"Yeah, that'll be best."

She searched his face for clues, he didn't make eye contact.

She shovelled her dignity from the floor and threw two pound coins on the table.

She left quickly, before she'd make a show of herself, either crying with confusion or head butting him.

The head butting would be good, but, she thought he just might hit her back.

She got a taxi and when it left her at the flat she hesitated, wondering if she should hang around and wait, surely there was an explanation for such bizzare behaviour? Sod it, she was going home. When she drove on to the main road she saw him coming, head down, hands in pockets, and looking so very lost. Margaret slowed down, but, not knowing what to say she drove on. She played a tape he had given her, old fashioned, crooners. "I thought you'd like this, my Ma liked it, you remind me of my Ma." Margaret had seen a photograph of the long deceased 'Ma' and was not flattered.

Tears blinded her, she pulled into a lay-by. Her mobile 'phone rang. It was him. "Where are you?"

"On my way home."

"Come on back, don't be daft."

"I don't want to come back, I can't stand the atmosphere, the crazy behaviour, everything changing from one minute to the next."

"Catch yourself on, it was only a bit of a joke."

"Well I'm not laughing."

"Remember, Mags you could be living with Mr Stitt."

Mr Stitt, lived in a ghetto in Belfast and apparently kept a sword on the wall which he swung wildly about, to instil order in his household. She laughed her head of at this story, but, not now.

Silence.

"Whatever you like," he said and put the 'phone down.

She drove on, went into the empty house, made coffee and took it to the garden.

Restless, she wandered about the house, veering from anger to smiling at something foolish he had said.

She was not ready to let this go.

She had a bath.

"Bathing again!" he would have said.

She lay back and looked round. He was right, it did look like a chemist shop.

She took a tray to bed, snack things, it was nine o'clock and she was exhausted. An emotional weariness, not tired enough to sleep. He'd 'phoned six times that night. She didn't answer.

The next day she set out her clothes for work, sorted out files to take. She spoke to no one and wandered from the house to the garden. She ate cheese on toast, drank too much coffee and felt that she had entered a surreal world. She went to bed, tried to read a book, couldn't take it in and fell asleep with the light on. She wakened at five am lying there going over things in her head. The tenderness, the laughter, the silences, the heavy toxic atmospheres. This did not make sense. She drove to work, she couldn't face breakfast.

"Morning, Margaret, the new group are in the kitchen and your programme for the day is in the training room," said the receptionist. Margaret thanked her and inwardly groaned at the prospect of a new and challenging group.

"Good morning, you may remember me from your interview, I'm Margaret, and when you've finished your tea, please come to the training room, which is opposite the reception area. Will we say five minutes?"

Ten faces looked blankly back, "Is that okay, everyone?"

"Yea, Mrs. We'll be there," Mr Tough guy had already established himself as leader of the pack.

So, she got through the day. Ice breakers, family history, hopes and dreams.

Finishing at four Margaret went into reception.

"Margaret, George 'phoned and asked you to call him back, you know George Alison?"

"Yes, yes, thank you."

She 'phoned unsure of what to say, she needed have fretted, he jumped right in.

"Hello, Mag's, you took your time, what do you want for your tea?"

"Is that it, do we not need to talk about what happened?"

"I'm making egg and chips so hurry up."

She drove across down, parked the car, and pressed the intercom, "Hello, it's me."

"Come on up."

Margaret went in to the flat, he thrust a bunch of quite nice lilies at her. "These flawers are for you."

"Thank you."

"Sit down now, you'll have it on yer knee 'til we get a table."

She knew she should not have returned, this was truly head melting stuff. This was also the 'green light' moment.

The go ahead for whatever would follow. Did she know this? Probably, on some level. But ....NO, no 'buts' no excuses, that's all past now.

'Old Margaret' as she thought of herself during this visit, shifted about, then pulled herself up and made her way to the bathroom. She wondered if there was a blanket or cushion to sit on. She looked in the hot press, and oh joy, there was a pillow. She sniffed it, smiling, he had teased her for "Always smelling things." Fusty and a bit mildewed but, it would do.

She returned to the garden and back to her memories.

She stayed, and felt at times like an unwanted guest at a party. A party she had looked forward to, and dressed her best for. Pretending it was fine, when, in reality it was far from it. She began to question her perceptions, making allowances, trying to make sense of non sense. As the mountain climber sees all of the mountain from the ground, so she could only survey the whole mess from a distance but, not while 'on the mountain'.

She encouraged him to move to a rented house with the

potential to buy. This house. She 'helped' him with his college work, often writing most of the assignment herself, it was easier. Oh, how he expanded with his importance whilst she diminished, becoming a version of herself which she hardly recognised. Friends she saw seldom. She hadn't the energy.

In the midst of the pain there was also immense pleasure. She would never forget being read to in bed.

'The smell of dusty cretonne, she was tired,' Joyce?" 'The Dubliners.' The baths he ran for her, the snacks and teas he made. They wandered about auctions and car boot sales, buying tat that could be made into something for the house he rented. Taking a train to stay in a seaside town, George with a plastic bag, clanking and clinking.

"What on earth have you got in that bag?" she asked, laughing.

"That smelly stuff you like, you know 'oils'."

"What else?"

"A wee radio, candles and sweets for later."

This was part of the George she loved, unsophisticated, endearing, and child like.

She could hardly bear to remember other holidays. Fraught with doom and an underlying sense of menace.

They went to Spain, Croatia, Greece, Canada, Italy, Scotland and Donegal. Some good times, but, they did not compensate for his sulks and endless demands. It is so wasteful and sad to think of it now. Everything had to revolve around George, he would get annoyed about something trivial and withdraw. How mean and absolute were those withdrawals, overshadowing what could have been wonderful whole experiences.

Often it was kinder to herself to let things go unchallenged. Making huge concessions.

Bit by bit, drip, drip, drip.

This reminded Margaret of 'The Billy Goats' gruff.' Clip, clip, clip over the bridge. She always did find that story threatening.

In the background were his seldom seen children, all with 'issues'. Margaret could not re-visit that. Trying to be 'inclusive' and make friends. Always going the extra mile. Grumpy wee people, always wanting more. No, this was about honouring the relationship, the good and the bad. The ugly.

When one area of your life is a mess that mess spills

over into other areas. And so it was with Margaret, before long she lost her job. A job she loved and was good at. She was challenged by people she did not respect, and already stretched, she simply walked out. She went to him seeking solace, but true to form, he was busy sorting out his college classes. She wept for her loss and then became busy. There was work to do in George's house.

Gone was the hideous suite from the flat and in place was a burgundy sofa, a small rocking chair, a book case and a small side table which Margaret transported from her own house. Prints on the walls and the kitchen decorated in cream and terracotta with checked curtains and a big notice board to keep track of George's important engagements. He saw no irony in this for he had become in his own estimation a man of substance. A mature(?) student with property. With his grant and benefits he was quite well off. He handed out a few pound coins to her, for 'women's things and bus fares'. She cringed to think of it. George blossomed. He was now the focus of all her nurturing and attention. He reminded her of 'Toad of Toad Hall' stomping about in fancy clothes and full of his own importance.

There was still some pleasure in all this home making. Decorating the bedrooms. Theirs became a heaven and a hell. For all the wonderful times, watching old black and white films, discussions, "What shall we talk about, you George?" she teased him. "Yes lets talk about ME," and so it was. Do not forget those fall outs in the bedroom, 'old Margaret' reminded herself. The fall outs, what else could she call them? Those which led to her clinging to the side of the bed, cold rigid and unforgiving. Silences in the morning. One or other of them stating, "We need to talk." How she dreaded those talks, and in fairness he probably did too. Despite the promises and intentions, nothing changed, or if they did it was for the worse. How many times had she packed her things? Toing and froing, up the road and down the road. It was all so wearisome and became predictable. She would drag a bit of strength from deep within her, and there he would be begging and pleading, sending beautiful cards and bouquets. When she had hardly tuppence to bless herself!

Margaret was not a woman without insight. She knew that she was stubborn, scathing and could rant and rave. She knew that she was not without her flaws, but, she knew that she had many strong characteristics. She was kind and generous, fun, but now she did not even recognise those positive traits. George was fractured in a way that she simply could not understand. Goodwill gestures were used as covert bartering, displeasure equalled withdrawal, tantrums, and challenges were met with 'talks' which endured for hours. Into this mix he administered many loving acts, he warmed her feet, tucked her hand into his pocket, fixed her hair, then – wham! She would inadvertently commit some blunder, it could be anything, wearing jeans which he condemned as too tight/young/unflattering. Spending too much time on the 'phone, not paying him enough attention. Endless demands. So much time spent rewinding incidents to try and identify her offences.

She had to move now, before he completely immobilised her.

Eventually, Margaret got a new job.

George was seething, and out he came in his full glory. Nasty, repellent traits, which she was recognising as lurking under the surface and just waiting to pounce.

"I suppose you'll be the boss in this tuppence halfpenny joint?"

"Yes, I will."

"Well, if you're the boss, what about me?"

"What about you?"

"Couldn't you get me a start?"

It was at that point when Margaret began to make her exit plans.

She knew that she would have to move house, and somewhere that he could not easily get to.

She went to the building society to explore her options.

Thus, began her house search, stealthily. She used the computer in work. Made an appointment to see a house with a dear friend and 'bingo'.

This move would not happen on his turf, he would go ballistic. Margaret was gleeful.

Those memories would keep for another day.

'Old Margaret' opened her eyes, it was cold now. She moved toward the house, leaving the pillow outside, in a small show of defiance. She went back upstairs and in an act which was voluntary she knelt on the floor and clasped her hands in prayer. Silently she gave thanks and sent a prayer that God would help George. She never could, and sadly she recognised what her trying had cost her. How arrogant she had been.

Margaret got to her feet, and went back down the stairs.

She stepped outside and pulled the door shut, putting

the key into a large padded envelope, which she would post to the solicitor tomorrow.

Margaret got into her car and drove away.

She did not need to look back.

PETER

I'm the oldest, I've two full brothers and a half brother and sister. My Dad did his best, but, when we were kids he was in and out of our lives. He'd ways of entertaining himself, know what I mean? Drinking, betting and chasing. He'd a way with the ladies, can't see why, well you don't see your Dad in that way, do you? When he was there he was alright, know what I mean? I better stop saying that. Bloody Margaret. "Surplus to requirements, let's assume we do indeed know what you mean."

I'm a bit ahead, losing the run of myself, I'm that eager to tell my story. Not many wants to hear it any more.

Here's the thing, Mum got fed up with it all and kicked

him out. I was sitting on the stairs listening, I did that a lot.

Weird, know what I mean? Sorry, I forgot. The writer woman is going to 'proof read' this but leave 'the essence in'. Wants to hear it in my voice, natural, like. Anyway, some woman had been round telling Mum in detail how my Dad had been entertaining himself with her. I must have been about ten at the time, couldn't understand all of it, but, enough. I was a street wise kid, well you had to be living on that estate. Mum told him that she'd had it up to her tits with his shenanigans. That was it. She wanted him out. I was scared, what would happen to me and the brothers? I mind thinking that. He was pleading, not like him, must have been drunk.

Then, he wasn't there any more. After a while he was living in somebody's caravan. We thought the caravan was great. Mum left us there a lot. She'd got a job, but, then he went on the drink and disappeared. After that he got a flat round the corner. I don't know where he'd been. Nobody told kids anything in them days.

I went off the rails, next thing I was in a home. 'Mal adjusted' was the label I got. I wrecked things, smashed furniture, broke other kids' toys even pulled curtains off the window. I heard a social worker saying, "Peter is acting out, learnt behaviour." I thought that made me important. I hate social workers, they're the worst.

Mum came to visit a few times, but, with the wee ones it was a bit of a trek. Dad came to see me, droning on and on, lecturing me – him! Sometimes I'd get him to play football with me, just to shut him up. Must have been in there about a year. They didn't know what to do with me. Said that I needed a safe and secure home environment. Right. Where was I going to get one of those? They live in la la land those social workers. Dad had got himself a new woman called Shauna. We were all to live with them. Wouldn't that be great? No it bleedin wouldn't, even I know that. Seems Mum had washed her hands of us all, she would have reasonable access. That didn't sound too hot. So, away we went to Shauna's place. Another housing estate, different flags, that's all. And us from the 'other side' – no bonfires or bands there.

It was phoney, us all trying to be like the bloody 'Walton's.' I loved them, the Walton's, all that 'Good night John Boy.' And people making cakes and doing things in big fields.

Before too long it was back to form. Different place same old same old. Him tearing down the sacred heart pictures, Shauna crying and "May Mother Mary and Saint Joseph forgive you." She said that a lot. I'll not tell you what he said. I'm supposed to keep the lingo clean.

Not too long after that I was away, in the remand home. No pulling down curtains there. No, Sir, they didn't put up with any shite. Sorry, nonsense. You'd be punished, not hit, no, those days were gone. Good thing, if you ask me some of them wardens were brutal bastards. No, it was subtle. Segregation, no 'association' they called it.

That meant no snooker, football or mixing with the others. You'd a died of boredom, a killer it was.

My Dad said that I had to learn to work the system. So, I did, but, my way. Thieving mostly.

They took us on trips once or twice, that was alright. I'd never been to the beach before. We whooped and ran wild, up and down the sand dunes, in and out of the sea.

Got myself a wee flat, had to see the probation officer every week. Not a bad bloke, had been a bad boy in his time. He'd 'turned it all around," said that I could do the same. Yeh, right. This was part of rehabilitation.

Rehabilitation to what? I'm not thick like that Margaret thought. Well, I don't know what she thought.

Bit off more that she could chew, I reckon.

I remember the first time I met her. Dad 'phoned and said that he thought it would be best to meet on neutral ground. What a laugh. He never said that, she did.

We met in a cafe in Botanic Avenue. I saw my Dad first, Jesus, he looked like a gangster or something. White shirt, jeans and a Crombie coat. Real fancy shoes. No tracky bottoms or polo shirts or trainers. I can't find the words for it, sort of 'shiny' he looked.

"This is Margaret, Peter." Except he didn't call her that, he called her 'Mags' always, I never heard anybody else call her that. Only him. I tried a few times, just to wind her up, but, it wasn't worth the aggro. "Are you my new Mommy?" I says, trying to be funny. She stood up and shook my hand, "I think you're a little old for a new Mommy and I don't want to be anyone's Mommy." That took the wind out of my sails.

"Have a big breakfast, Peter," says my Dad, before things went right off the track.

He was looking at her like he was about to go into a coma, and being all polite, and using big words.

Margaret excused herself to go to the toilet. Only she didn't really 'do' toilet, you couldn't imagine her – well never mind. I asked him, "Are you back on medication or what?"

"No, I've changed, I'm at university now, got my act together, and Mags won't stand for any nonsense."

Bully for her. We never did talk about things, him and me, not really. Football, horses, snooker, that sort of bloke talk. Safer. You could see he thought she was the dog's do das, let me tell you, she was no page three girl. God knows what fairy story he'd spun for her.

A few weeks later I was invited for tea, I wouldn't have bothered, but, I was hoping he would slip me a few quid and I could do with a feed. The gaffe was nice, but, it just wasn't him. Girly maybe, don't know, all blending and flowers and the table set properly. No shovelling a pizza down your neck in front of the telly. We'd home-made soup, then he went off to fetch 'the main,' as she called it. I thought he was away to the electric box, swear to God. In he came with this pasta stuff. Well, I know about pasta, living in the flat it's easy to cook, and cheap. But, him? Well, he was more a 'boil in the bag' man. Can't remember what the talk was. Seemed they were showing off. Oh, that's right – there was this brilliant thing that happened. I'll tell you later about that. Just remind me it's about the tights.

About ten she says, "Well I'm off to bed, I'll leave you to it." She leans over and kisses him and to me she says, "Safe journey," like I was going to the Himalayas', or maybe she was letting me know there was no spare bed for me. Off she clumped, bit heavy on her feet, not exactly dainty. Leaving him with all the dishes, "Give us a hand to clear this up, Peter."

"Do you rent this place?" He hesitated, "Course, I do, what? You think I could afford to buy?" I didn't know for years and years that she'd helped him to buy it. In his name too. Anyway it was all, Mags says this and Mags says that and plays and books and cinema. Holidays too, real fancy places. I thought maybe he was on uppers. I checked the cupboards, but, not a pill in sight. He got all huffy about that, "I know what you're looking for, and I'm not on anything."

Enthusiasm – that's the word, my Dad and her were suffering from a big dose of enthusiasm. He gave me a tenner, big deal, I'd earned it listening to those two.

I remember going to see me Grandpa. Grumpy old git he was, but, likeable. Straight, no conning him.

"What do you want?" or, "What brings you to these parts?" That's when you knew he'd got a bet up. I stuck the kettle on to make us a cuppa. "Rich tea under the counter, don't scoff them all, butter in the fridge." Good, a bit of telly, a bit of chat, normal. Then I saw the basket over beside the sink. One of those things you see on the telly or in the shops at Christmas. A hamper, that's it. Only it wasn't Christmas. I was just taking a closer look when he yells, "Don't touch my basket, I want to show it to the home help."

"Only looking, Grandpa."

A wee jar of marmalade, liquorice, nougat, after eights, all decorated with a big bow. Tasteful. Could only mean one thing. "Where'd you get it?" "Margaret brought it, came across town, out of her work. Just passing she told me, but, didn't want to make a fuss. Never comes with her two arms the one length."

He'd got the Margaret fever. I started to talk about the match, but, no, he'd important news to tell.

"Took me to a play the other night."

I dropped my tea.

"Now look what you've done, you bleeding' eejit, clean that up."

I couldn't help it. My Grandpa only went to the shops or the bookies, or at the weekend to the residents lounge to play bingo. I couldn't believe my ears, I was that shocked that's why I dropped the tea.

"The Lyric it was, I put on me best suit. Our George was there too. Collected at the door I was, and Margaret insisted he saw me in when we came back. A right night it was, nice wee blade, bit a gumption. Not like them other two eejits he married.

I didn't stay long, wait till I told our Willie all this. He was my brother, two years younger than me, right wee hard man. I 'phoned the remand home to see when I could visit.

We were in the visitors lounge, I'd brought him some stuff and he was having a good look to see if there was enough stuff to bargain with. I knew the ropes. "Thanks mate," then he gave me my opening, "Seen our Dad?"

I filled him in, even the Grandpa at a play. We pissed ourselves laughing.

"Do that voice again of Dad and the soup, go on, Peter."

"Well, he's sitting there like Lord Charles's dummy, remember that programme we loved with the dummy?

"All dressed up, like he's having dinner at the Europa. He attacks the soup, like he's never had a drop a soup in his natural and he says." I started to laugh again, 'cos I'd remembered about the tights. I straightened up.

"This soup is just delish, Mags pet."

"Delish? Him? He never!"

"Did too, I could hardly stop myself laughing out loud."

"You said on the 'phone you'd tell me something about tights?"

"Yea, I'd nearly forgotten that."

"Go on, go on," says the kid brother, wriggling in the seat, clapping his hands, all excited at the fun of these stories. "Well, he excuses himself, If you don't mind, come back in all smug and smiling all over his gob with this box."

"What size was the box?"

"Big, like one of those ones you see in the shop for crisps. Anyway, she's all smiles, "Oh George, for me?"

"Just a wee something I picked up in the market." Oh. Oh.

"She opens the box, packets and packets of tights. 'American tan' it says on the cellophane, well even I knew she wasn't an 'American tan' type of woman.

Should a seen the face on her, she opens the packet and pulls out the tights. One leg is about six foot long and the other leg wouldn't go on a doll." I couldn't hold it in. It was priceless.

"What'd she say? What'd she say?"

"What am I to do with these, George? Wear one leg as a scarf and the other as a mitten?"

"What'd Dad say?"

"He was mad – tore open loads of them, they were all the same. He was muttering about strangling the bastard who sold him them."

Our bellies were sore from laughing.

"It's as well you had the grub, he might have cleared the table!"

He hadn't met Margaret yet.

I left our Willie then, with his goodies and the stories to keep him going.

Five years later, he was dead. Drug overdose, only twenty-one. My Dad says he has five kids, I think he let on it didn't happen. 'Denial,' they call it.

Anyway, I better get a move on, he wants the writer

woman to read this to him before he snuffs it.

I 'phoned Shauna one day,

"How are you keeping, Peter?"

"Alright, and you and the kids Shauna?"

"Glad someone asks about them – George is jollying himself with his fancy woman. The two of them all over the place on luxury holidays."

I was in for a real ear bashing. She said that they took them out sometimes in 'the car' she said it like it was a space ship. She said they hated going out with them and their Daddy had gone all weird and dressed funny. They took them to places they didn't like and he threw them the odd fiver now and again. They called Margaret 'Cruella de Ville."

She asked me to come down some time, and I said that I'd see what I could do. We both knew it wouldn't happen. We were strangers really. I didn't know the wee ones, well, hardly at all. She wasn't a bad spud, Shauna, I felt a bit sorry for her stuck in that hole with hardly any money and two wee ones. We were all strangers in a way, I didn't get on with the other brother, Tom, sneaky wee brat. I avoided him when I could.

Next big thing to happen was the split. Well, I'd seen him in a bad way plenty of times. But, this was bad, top of the range bad. He hit the drink, was back on medication, and was in and out of A&E. Sitting with the street drinkers, throwing money around him. When he wasn't crying he was screaming and tearing at his hair. He didn't wash. That was bad, he always had a shower and a shave, no matter what. I didn't know what to do. I got him into a centre to dry out. The doctor said he was calling for someone. No prizes for guessing who. So I 'phoned her.

"Hello, Margaret, this is Peter, you know, George's son?"

"Yes, I know."

"Well, the thing is Dad's in hospital and he's asking for you."

"Well, the thing is, I've given your father everything I have to give, and quite frankly it was like pouring a lot of water into a big bucket with a hole in it. Nothing left to give. Goodbye."

I saw her in the papers, all her good works for 'lost causes.' Huh! My Dad never spoke her name again.

He was never the same either, like part of him wasn't there any more.

He sent all the furniture to the auction and closed up the house. Drifted about, didn't care where he lived.

He said "The light has gone out."

Well, silver cloud and all that, I'm sure we'll get a tidy penny for that house.

HIS STORY

Always had too much to say for herself, that Mags one. Many's the time I felt like giving her a good slap. I didn't, now, that's restraint. I heard that brother of hers had bitten off somebody's thumb in a fight. Don't get me wrong, I liked him, dead on, but she thought the sun shone out of his arse. Anyway, I wasn't going to give him an excuse to maybe bite off something of mine.

For starters, cooking for her was a nightmare, fresh this and no tins that. Far reared she was from olives, I can tell you. When I said that I didn't have time for all that, know what she said? "Off on an expedition to buy a wee loaf. What else would be on your agenda?" See what I mean? Mouthy. Imagine if my Ma had said things like that to my Da. Well, she wouldn't, knew better.

I'll tell you the truth, God knows what she's told you.

Probably along the lines of how great she was to me and what a blaggard I was. Am I right or am I right? I've nothing to lose, the old breathin' isn't so good. The Doc says we're looking at a few weeks – tops. Still, that Dame who comes to write all this stuff isn't hard to look at. Life in the old dog yet. Maybe a few quid for the kids. My Peter could do with a hand, so could the rest of them. Five I have, know what she said to that? "Didn't they have contraception where you lived?" Cheeky Mags, not nice sometimes. I can still hear her voice.

Miss 'fancy pants' needed a brood of kids round her, she wouldn't have time then for swanning off to them two bit jobs she thought were so important. Or going to the beauty parlour or buying fancy creams and scent. Don't get me started.

I'll take a wee break now, for the nebuliser, like.

That's better, now where was I? The writer woman says "Just let it flow," if I was out of this bed I'd show her flow! Ha, ha.

I'm a short bloke about five-five, but never hampered me with the ladies. Mags said that it was insulting and disrespectful the way I looked at women. Probably jealous. I was married twice well, marriages break down. No big deal. Couldn't get a job and I wasn't going to the shipyard every day like my Da. Do your head in. So we lived on the benefits, me getting the odd bet up now and then. Maybe a few hand outs from the in-laws. I suppose my drinking didn't help.

"Too far back, keep it relevant to Mags," says the writer woman. Bossy boots. Nice way of speaking, though, just like Mags. I loved her, Mags, not the writer woman, course I did. We had some great times and she's the one I measured against everybody. It was desperate the break up. Thought I'd be in the 'funny farm' for the rest of my days. "Not politically correct, George, no one says 'funny farm' any more."

Well I do.

So what attracted me in the first place? Well, she was a bit of a looker, but it was her attitude too. The cheek of her, which was great when you weren't involved in it. For example, sending things back, as cool as you like.

"I wonder could you replace this cup. It's cracked, you see." I thought she was cracked and I was cut, cut to the bone for the wee girl who was serving us.

Or another time that I remember, "This is not what I ordered, please bring another, without the dressing, thank you." I couldn't look at her when she did those things. Never took a fizz out of her. "I'm paying for what I want, not what someone else decides."

When she didn't like what I wore she'd make a snide comment, something she knew would stick in my nut, and put me right off. I'd these lovely shoes with a buckle. Cracker they were.

"Are you auditioning for the principle boy role in those shoes?" I never wore them again. She was funny too, I remember trying to put together a clothes rail, screws everywhere and instructions, and bits left over. On her way through to the kitchen she glanced at me and said, "I believe they're looking for riveters in the shipyard, George." Stomping off in her big boots to make that fancy coffee. I laughed that much the thing collapsed round me.

She was good with the kids at the start, well, for a few years really. Out for picnics, she was the hell for picnics, the pictures, the museum, loads of things. Made a lot of effort, but it wasn't what they were used to, she was too different for their liking. Anyway, after a while she stopped, she said that we'd pushed her to the wire. Don't ask me what she meant.

Clever too, never just gave you an answer off the cuff. I remember asking her once if she was happy, simple, right. Not with her, "Well, I think you need to be not too intelligent to be happy all the time, there are moments, of course. Anyway no one wants to be a laughing lunatic." I tried not to laugh.

The first time we went away was to Donegal, I'd never been, she thought it was wonderful. I just liked being with her, never mind the scenery or the deedle-e-dee music. I loved talking with her then, it was interesting, yeh that's what it was, made me think. She gave me confidence, but, I gave her loads too. She was a bit buttoned up when I met her, like she'd lived in a convent or something, but, she loosened up with me. We were spontaneous together. Liked the old films, and music, went to loads of things, plays and recitals – the kids thought I'd lost the plot. I heard Peter telling his brother, "My Da's away on a soiree with your woman, dare say we'll not be invited," dead droll, didn't know he even knew the word 'soiree'. Anyway we lived a lot, and hurt a lot, not just her, I did too. We'd special times, snuggling up in bed, reading and singing. She couldn't sing a note. We'd guess songs, like children and laugh. She'd cold, cold feet. Funny the things you remember. We'd dance in the house and she'd laugh her head off when I'd shake my bum at her. Real belly laughs.

She hated me sulking, I didn't like it either. Sometimes I

knew why and sometimes I didn't. I might have lost a lot of money in the bookies, I wouldn't tell her that. Told her I did the odd accumulator. It might have been the boys' as she'd called my kids, getting into trouble. Maybe I was trying to be something I wasn't. Or us arguing, or her not giving us a hand with the assignments. I went right in on myself at those times, didn't want to speak, then couldn't. She used to ask me what was wrong then she stopped. Irrational that's what it was. One time I tried after we'd been rowing I told her that my Ma and Da would make up by him making her a cup of tea. I'll never forget what she said to that, "Would he offer the tea before or after he broke her nose?" Nasty. Yet, my Da thought she was the bee's knees. Took him to a play about snooker, made a bit of a fuss of him, he said that she was my backbone. She didn't like that, "Why, have you not got your own backbone?" She stuck up for me loads and I thought we'd be together for ever.

Loyalty – that was another thing she put great store by. Did she mean faithful? ("Give or take a night or two" as the old drone she liked to listen to sang, can't remember his name). No loyal, standing side by side was what she meant – even bought a poem about it, framed and on the wall, didn't even ask my permission. I took it down off the wall and jumped on it. She was terrified, but, defiant, as usual, "Not very attractive, George."

It was great getting to the University, I was chuffed with myself. I know she helped me at the beginning, but, I could tell she didn't want to. Said that I kept her out of bed and she had to get up for work. I started to do other modules, that's what they called them, and she hadn't a clue. Said that the cold war bored her. The house was homely, I'll give her that. Warm and comfortable. If the walls could talk! I heard somebody talking in the bookies about re-mortgaging, couldn't believe it, and sounded like money from America. Off I went, and before I knew it I had big money in the bank. It went to my head and I took to the drink.

That was the beginning of the end. I don't want to think about that. Mag's weeping and wailing, me throwing her clothes out on the street, me on medication, again. What a nightmare, black-outs the heap. We met up loads of times, I dreaded those words, "Do you want to meet up, George?" No, I didn't. I wanted to get off my face. I'd had it with proper and structure and manners and baths, and all that shite.

She came one day to get her clothes and all those witch's potions.

Her brother was with her, he never spoke.

"I'm leaving, I've bought a house, no forwarding address."

I was gob smacked, mortified in front of the brother.

I phoned her later, drunk. She put the 'phone down. I suppose I 'phoned her a lot. I don't remember.

She agreed to meet me about two months later, only if I was sober. I was, just.

The last time I saw her, we were going up the tow path, I felt like pushing her in, or jumping in myself.

The Doc had said that I was depressed, I told her that, she didn't even reply. I told her that I had locked up the house and given the key to the solicitor and given him power of attorney.

"That's good, keeps things right," she said.

"Right? Do you know I'm going to the psychiatric ward tomorrow and I don't give a shite about speaking right or nice or money or books or pleasant smells or bloody olives either," I was shouting into her face.

She leaned over and stroked my face, tears spouting down her face, she turned and walked away, hunched over, forlorn, lost really. Vulnerable, I loved her best when she was vulnerable.

I know she'll go back to the house, I never did – my back bone didn't go that far.

You were right about some things, not all, mind. There are moments, things you take with you. Like that tender stroke to my face.

"Go gentle into that good night." You'll have to hang about a while longer, Mags.

ABOUT THE AUTHOR

Jacqueline McClenaghan is a graduate of Queens University Belfast. Her writing is influenced by her role as a professional counsellor working with the homeless as well as those involved with drug and alcohol misuse and survivors of domestic abuse. In the past Jacqueline was a member of a local writing group. She lives in County Down, although would admit to being a 'blow-in'.

Your Shame My Shame

Printed in Poland
by Amazon Fulfillment
Poland Sp. z o.o., Wrocław